Jeff stopped in front of one of the cages. "This is the pup I was talking about," he explained. "His name is Alfie."

Anna took a deep breath and peeked into the cage. Inside was a tiny brown-and-black puppy. He was so small that she could probably pick him up with one hand! He had wiry fur and shining black eyes, and as soon as he saw Anna, his tail started wagging.

"He's a three-month-old Border terrier," Jeff explained. Anna knew that Jeff was talking, but she couldn't tear her eyes away from the tiny dog. "They are a small breed of dog anyway, but Alfie here is especially tiny – he must have been the runt of the litter. Would you like to go in?"

Anna nodded wordlessly. She felt so excited she could hardly breathe. Jeff unlocked the cage and held the door so that Anna and her mum could slip in.

Anna looked at Alfie and her breath caught in her throat. *Please like me*, she thought desperately. She knelt down on the floor, and Alfie rushed straight over to her. He sniffed her legs and then jumped up onto her lap! Anna gave a shaky sigh and beamed at Mum, who smiled at them both.

Have you read all these books in the
Battersea Dogs & Cats Home series?

ALFIE'S
story

by
Sarah Hawkins

Illustrated by Artful Doodlers
Puzzle illustrations by Jason Chapman

RED FOX

BATTERSEA DOGS & CATS HOME: ALFIE'S STORY
A RED FOX BOOK 978 1 849 41412 8

First published in Great Britain by Red Fox,
an imprint of Random House Children's Books
A Random House Group Company

This edition published 2011

1 3 5 7 9 10 8 6 4 2

The Random House Group Limited supports the Forest Stewardship Council®
(FSC®), the leading international forest certification organisation. All our
titles that are printed on Greenpeace approved FSC® certified paper carry the
FSC® logo. Our paper procurement policy can be found
atwww.randomhouse.co.uk/environment

MIX
Paper from
responsible sources
FSC® C016897

Set in 13/20 Stone Informal

Red Fox Books are published by Random House Children's Books,
61–63 Uxbridge Road, London W5 5SA

www.**kids**at**randomhouse**.co.uk
www.**totallyrandombooks**.co.uk
www.**randomhouse**.co.uk

Addresses for companies within The Random House Group Limited
can be found at: www.randomhouse.co.uk/offices.htm

THE RANDOM HOUSE GROUP Limited Reg. No. 954009

A CIP catalogue record for this book is available from the British Library.

Printed and bound in Great Britain by
CPI Bookmarque, Croydon, CR0 4TD

Turn to page 93 for lots
of information on
Battersea Dogs & Cats Home,
plus some cool activities!

Meet the stars of the Battersea Dogs & Cats Home series to date . . .

Bailey

Misty

Chester

Rusty

Daisy

Max

Snowy

Stella

Huey

Angel

Cosmo

Alfie

Coco

A New Friend

Anna giggled into the phone as she listened to her best friend. "And then the donkey knocked over the stall and started *eating* all the vegetables!" Sophie told her.

"Then what did it do?" Anna asked eagerly. All kinds of exciting things had happened to Sophie since she'd moved to a little village in France two weeks ago.

Sophie used to live in the house next door to Anna, and they'd gone to the same nursery and been in the same class at school, too. They went to Rainbows and Brownies together, and spent so much time at each other's houses that Anna's mum joked that  Sophie was more like Anna's sister than her best friend. But when Sophie's parents decided to move back to France, where Sophie's mum grew up, there was nothing Anna or Sophie could do. Anna had spent every second of the summer holidays with her friend, but all too soon she was helping Sophie pack the last of her things into boxes. Sophie had given Anna her favourite cuddly toy, a unicorn called Magic, for her to keep.

Anna grabbed Magic and held him tight. For the past two weeks all she'd been able to do was talk to Sophie on the phone. They called each other every Friday, but it was still funny not being able to talk to Sophie every day.

Because it was
still the
holidays, she
and Mum
had done
lots of fun
things
together
and Anna
had been
able to pretend
that Sophie was
just away for a
couple of weeks and that she was coming
back. Anna's tummy turned over. She
was going to miss Sophie even more
when school started again on Monday
and she had to go without her.

"It was so funny, Anna Banana, you
should have been there!" Sophie laughed.

Anna giggled, but she was getting that
sad achy feeling again in her tummy.
Everything was new and exciting for
Sophie, she had a brand-new bedroom, a
new school, new friends and even a new
language to learn. But for Anna,
everything she did just reminded her that
Sophie wasn't there any more. The worst
thing of all was
that there was
no one to talk
to. Everyone
else already
had their
best friend
at school,
and there
wasn't
anyone left
for Anna.

She wanted to join in with the groups of girls who played games at break time, but she found it really hard to talk to people she didn't know well. It was fine when Sophie was there because she would talk to anyone as if she'd known them her whole life, while Anna hung back until she was sure they were nice. Anna just couldn't help feeling like she'd been left behind.

Just then Anna's mum put her head round the bedroom door and waved. "Time to say goodbye," she mouthed.

"I've got to go, Soph," Anna said. "Talk to you next Friday."

"OK," Sophie said sadly. "Miss you."

"Miss you too." Anna heard the click as Sophie put the phone down, and swallowed. There seemed to be a hard lump in her throat.

"You could have talked to her for a *little* bit longer," Mum said, coming to sit next to her on the bed.

"It's not the same," Anna cried, taking off her glasses and wiping away the tears that had sprung to her eyes. "I just wish she hadn't gone!"

"Oh, Banana," Mum said. "I know it's been tough for you. Change is always hard. And I know it doesn't feel like it now, but change can be good too."

Anna wasn't convinced. Change always seemed to be sad – and scary. First there was her dad moving to his own house and living with Laura, who talked to Anna like she was a baby and got cross about stupid little things. Then there was Laura and Dad announcing that Anna was going to have a little brother. Anna liked Sam now, but when Laura and Dad

had first told her
about it she'd
felt like Dad
had got a
brand new
family
without her.
And then
Sophie's family
had changed
everything again when

they'd moved to France.

Change was not

good at all.

"So what do you think?" Mum asked, looking at Anna excitedly.

"About what?" Anna asked.

Mum shook her head. "Have you been daydreaming again? About getting a puppy! It'd take your mind off Sophie, and it'd give me some company when you spend weekends at your dad's house."

"A puppy?" Anna's mouth fell open. Mum's change was a *puppy*? Anna's thoughts raced. She could take a puppy for walks, and stroke it, and teach it tricks. Dogs were meant to be people's best friends, weren't they? If she had a puppy best friend maybe she wouldn't miss her human one so much!

"Well?" Mum asked again.

Anna flung her arms around her so hard that her glasses bumped against Mum's jumper and she had to take them off again.

"Is that a yes?" Mum laughed.

Anna could barely speak, she just nodded frantically. "Oh!" she squealed. "I can't wait to tell Sophie!"

Meeting Alfie

The next morning Anna sat on the stairs impatiently and traced her fingers round the red buttons on her coat. She'd got up really early and had been dressed for ages, but Mum still wasn't ready.

Last night Mum had told her that they were going to get the puppy from a place called Battersea Dogs & Cats Home, where they found nice homes for cats and

dogs that didn't have families of their
own. Anna had wanted to go straight
away, before Mum could change her
mind, but Mum had told her that it was
a bit too late to make the journey then –
but they'd go the very next day. Anna
and Mum had spent the rest of the
evening looking at the Battersea Dogs &
Cats Home website and
searching through all
the dogs that were
up for adoption.

There were so many different kinds. Anna had felt a bit sad that they all needed happy homes – but at least there would soon be one less!

"Come on, Mum!" Anna called up the stairs for what felt like the hundredth time.

Mum came out of her bedroom and gave an exaggerated sigh. "Darling, they're not going to run out of dogs!" she laughed as she came down the stairs.

"I know, but I just can't wait any longer!" Anna said, jumping up to give Mum her coat and propelling her towards the door.

"I haven't even had any breakfast!" Mum grumbled.

"I made you toast!" Anna pointed to a plate on the stairs. "You can eat as we go."

"OK, OK!" Mum laughed. "Where are the car keys?"

"Here!" Anna held them up. "*Now* can we go, *please!*"

*

It took an hour to drive down to
Battersea, and Anna got more and more
excited as they went. "Look out for the
sign!" Mum told her as they got closer.
Anna pressed her face up to the window,
searching for the blue circle with the cat
and the dog curled up together.

"There it is!" she
shouted, jumping
up and down
in her
seat.

Mum parked nearby and they walked back to the Home. Well, Mum walked while Anna raced ahead. Her feet were too excited to walk!

When they got to the reception they were met by a tall man who grinned at them and told them his name was Jeff. Mum explained that they had come to get a puppy of their very own.

"Well that's exciting!" Jeff smiled as he took them through to a little room. "I'm just going to ask you some questions to make sure we get the perfect pup for you. What kind of dog are you looking for?" he asked Anna. Anna felt her cheeks go hot, and she bent her head forward so that her hair hid her face. Jeff looked from her to Mum, and Mum answered.

"We'd like a little dog. We don't have a very large house as it's only the two of us, so we need a puppy that's not going to grow too big."

"And what do you want, Anna?" Jeff asked. Anna felt her face go hot again. She didn't know what to say, so she just looked at Mum.

"Anna wants a friendly dog, don't you?" Mum said for her. Anna nodded.

"Well, I think I know just the pup for you!" Jeff declared. "And he's a quiet one too," he said with a wink that made Anna go even redder.

Jeff led them
though a big set of
doors into the
dog kennels.
There were huge
ramps leading up to
different levels, and they

followed Jeff up two
floors before he
took them into a
room with cages
down each side.
As they passed by,
all the dogs barked, and
Anna peeked into each
cage. There were
huge dogs that
gave big WOOFS
and smaller
yappy ones.

They were all nice, but they weren't what
Anna imagined when she thought of *her*
dog. None of them were quite right
somehow. Anna felt sure that she'd know
her puppy as soon as she saw it!

Suddenly Jeff stopped
in front of one of
the cages. "This
is the pup I
was talking
about," he
explained.
"His name
is Alfie."

Anna took a deep breath and peeked into the cage. Inside was a tiny brown-and-black puppy. He was so small that she could probably pick him up with one hand! He had wiry fur and shining black eyes, and as soon as he saw Anna, his tail started wagging.

"He's a three-month-old Border terrier," Jeff explained. Anna knew that Jeff was talking, but she couldn't tear her eyes away from the tiny dog. "They are a small breed of dog anyway, but Alfie here is especially tiny – he must have been the runt of the litter. Would you like to go in?"

Anna nodded wordlessly. She felt so excited she could hardly breathe. Jeff unlocked the cage and held the door so that Anna and her mum could slip in.

Anna looked at Alfie and her breath caught in her throat. *Please like me*, she thought desperately. She knelt down on the floor, and Alfie rushed straight over to her. He sniffed her legs and then jumped up onto her lap! Anna gave a shaky sigh and beamed at Mum, who smiled at them both.

Anna stroked Alfie as they both sat
quietly. Unlike all the
other dogs, Alfie
didn't bark at
all, but he
wagged his tail
so hard from
side to side it
looked like he'd
fall over!

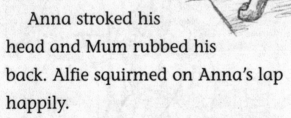

Anna stroked his
head and Mum rubbed his
back. Alfie squirmed on Anna's lap
happily.

"I told you he's quiet," Jeff smiled.
"I've never heard him bark."

Anna smiled. *He's just like me!* she
thought. Mum must have been thinking
the same because she caught Anna's eye
and grinned.

"What do you think?" Mum whispered. "Is he the puppy for us?"

This time Anna knew just what to say. "Yes," she breathed. "Oh, yes *please*!"

Puppy Time!

Anna sighed with happiness as she put
the final touches on her painting. She'd
drawn a picture of Alfie, his shiny black
eyes peeking out from his brown and
black fur, and a big doggy grin on his
cheeky face. It wasn't anywhere near as
cute as he was in real life, but it had been
fun to do.

She'd waited for two whole weeks, but

today was finally the
day that Alfie was
coming to live
with them!
After school
she and Mum
were going
back to
Battersea,
and bringing
Alfie home!
Before he had
been allowed
home, someone
from Battersea
had come round and
checked that their house was a nice place
for him to live. Anna had been worried
that it would be ages before they came,
but it had only taken a couple of days.

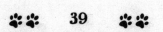

Mum had stayed home from work and showed them round – not that it had taken long in their tiny house. They'd said that everything was fine, and Mum and Anna could come and get Alfie as soon as they were ready.

Every time Anna thought about the little pup she felt her tummy fizz with excitement. She was just painting WELCOME HOME ALFIE in big letters at the top of the picture, when there was a voice from behind her. "Oh!" it said, making Anna jump. Anna turned to see Tamsin, a girl from her class, looking at her drawing. "Is that a puppy?" Tamsin asked.

"This is Alfie," said Anna. "He's sort of my puppy. I mean, I haven't got him yet, but I'm going to get him today. I'm making this poster for when he arrives."

"Oh, wow! That's so cool!" Tamsin grinned. "I'd *love* to have a puppy! I've got a hamster but I can't take *him* for walks. You're so lucky."

"I know!" Anna sighed. "He's the sweetest puppy you've ever seen – he's so tiny, and he's got such big eyes and a cute little nose!" Anna started describing how Alfie had sat on her lap in Battersea while Tamsin oohed and ahhed.

"I want to meet him!" Tamsin said as the bell went. "Promise you'll bring him into school one day?"

"I promise," Anna smiled. Tamsin rushed away to pack up her art things and Anna suddenly felt funny. She couldn't believe she'd talked so much. When she was telling Tamsin about Alfie she hadn't felt shy at all!

"Home time!" the teacher called.

Anna packed up her things as fast as she could. Holding her poster out in front of her so she didn't smudge the wet paint, she rushed out to Mum's car.

It wasn't home time, it was puppy time!

Alfie Arrives

When they got to Battersea, Mum filled out some paperwork in the reception while Anna waited impatiently. Then Jeff appeared with Alfie trotting behind him. Alfie raced right over to Anna, his tail wagging like crazy. Anna laughed and bent down to stroke him.

"I know it's silly because I've only met you once," she whispered into his fur, "but I've missed you so much!" Alfie jumped up onto her lap and nuzzled into her chest. He'd missed her too! "We're never going to be apart again!" Anna smiled at him. "You're going to live with us forever!" Alfie looked up at her and he panted slightly, his mouth curved into a doggy grin.

While Mum finished sorting
everything out, Anna played with Alfie.
The tiny dog was so excited that he raced
around, and galloped over to the little
shop at the side of the reception. The lady
at the till laughed and
leaned over to look
at the little puppy
scampering
about the
shop, sniffing
everything.

"Done!"
Mum
announced
as she came
over. "You
officially belong to us, Alfie!"

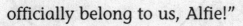

Anna grinned in delight, and Alfie's
tail wagged even harder.

"Mum, can we buy him something?" Anna asked.

"Oh yes, let's have a look," Mum said. "We've already got most things that he needs though." Anna thought about the new basket, bowl and lead all waiting for Alfie at home.

"We haven't got him any toys yet," she  said, looking up at a rack full of catnip mice and balls. Anna picked up a toy bone and it gave a loud "*squeak!*" Alfie's ears perked up and he jumped at her legs excitedly. "He likes it!" Anna laughed.

"Go on then," Mum said. "We'll get
him that as well. He's already spoilt
rotten – and we haven't even got him
home yet!"

On the way home Anna sat in the
back and held Alfie. She couldn't take her
eyes off the tiny puppy on her lap. She
stroked his fur and felt his velvety-soft
ears and damp black nose. Alfie
loved all the attention,
and sat happily on
her lap, nibbling
at his toy bone,
which made
soft squeaking
noises.

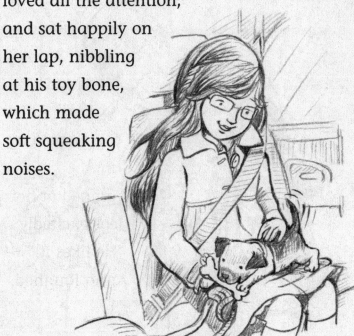

As they pulled into their driveway, Anna's tummy rumbled so loudly that Alfie looked at it suspiciously, as if there was an animal underneath her school shirt.

"Oh no!" Mum giggled. "It's a bit past dinner time, isn't it! You carry Alfie in and I'll go and get on with dinner."

Mum opened the front door and Anna carefully carried Alfie inside.

"Welcome home, Alfie!" Anna cried, putting him down and waving her poster for him to see. Alfie started trotting about, rushing from the sofa to the door and sniffing everywhere.

"Come on, Alfie, I'll show you where your things are!" Anna patted her legs and Alfie scampered towards her, squeaking the toy bone he was holding in his mouth.

"Well!" Mum said, as Anna and Alfie came bounding into the kitchen. "For a dog that doesn't bark, you certainly make quite a racket!" The toy bone squeaked again as Alfie scratched round the sides of his basket, then jumped in and flopped down happily. His tail was still wagging from side to side. Anna didn't think that it had stopped moving since they'd picked him up!

Anna put a bowl of water down for him, and Mum opened a can of dog food and spooned it into his bowl. Then she spooned soup from a can into bowls for her and Anna and popped them in the microwave. "I'd better not get the tins mixed up!" she joked.

Mum and Anna sat at the little kitchen table and watched Alfie as he tucked into his food. He was so tiny he could almost have fitted into the bowl!

Anna gulped down her soup. Once
she'd finished, she sat down next to
the basket and stroked Alfie's fur.
He wriggled in delight,
turning on his back so
she could

give him a tummy rub. "Why do you think he doesn't talk, Mum?" Anna asked.

"Well, the people at Battersea said there's nothing wrong with his voice. He *could* bark, he just doesn't. He's certainly a clever little dog, and it's OK to be a bit quiet. Some of my favourite people don't say very much," she grinned.

Anna gave a little smile and pushed her glasses up her nose. "He is happy though, isn't he?" she added.

"Of course he is! Just look at his waggy tail!" Mum laughed. "I don't think I've ever seen a happier little pup."

"*Squeaker-squeak!*" went the toy bone as Alfie stretched out for another tummy tickle.

Suddenly there was a shrill ring. Alfie leaped up, his ears twitching. He ran over to the phone and stood underneath it, looking at Anna and Mum expectantly.

"That's the phone, Alfie," Anna explained.

"Oh! It's Friday – it must be Sophie! I completely forgot!" Anna answered the phone. "Hi, Sophie! Hold on one sec."

Anna held the
phone under
her chin so
that she could
pick up Alfie
too and take
them both
upstairs. It
was a good
thing he was
so small!

"This is my
room, Alfie,"
she said as
they went
inside. Her
bedroom was very small too, and there
was only just enough room to walk
between the bed and the wardrobe, but
she and Mum had made it really cosy.

There was a shelf above her bed with all
her books on it, and the walls were
painted Anna's favourite shade of green.
Anna put Alfie down on the bed and he
wandered over to sniff Magic the unicorn
and Anna's other soft toys. Anna sat
down next to him and he jumped
into her lap and
nuzzled his nose
under her
arm.

"Sorry, Soph, I was just getting Alfie sorted," Anna explained.

"Ooooh, is he there?" Sophie squealed. "I can*not* believe you've got a puppy!"

Anna stroked Alfie's soft black ears. "I know. It's amazing! We've just brought him home from Battersea. He's so lovely, and the best thing, Soph, is that he's quiet, just like me. He doesn't bark at all!" Anna told her friend all about Alfie. Usually Sophie talked and Anna listened, but tonight it was the other way round!

Sophie was really pleased for Anna and asked loads of questions about Alfie.

"Send me photos!" she pleaded. "I wish I could see him in real life."

"I wish you were here too," Anna agreed. "We could have had so much fun together with Alfie."

When she finally put the phone down, Anna looked at Alfie. The little puppy rolled onto his back for a tummy rub and Anna laughed. It seemed strange that it was only a few weeks ago that she'd spoken to Sophie and felt so sad. With Alfie around, Anna didn't think she'd ever be miserable again!

A Horrible Announcement

Anna played with Alfie all weekend, and had the most fun she'd had since Sophie left. But on Sunday night she still felt nervous about going to school the next day. She wished she could take Alfie with her so she'd have someone to talk to at playtime, and someone to eat her sandwiches with. Since Sophie had gone,

Anna had been so shy about eating lunch with people she didn't know, she'd been eating really quickly and then going out to the playground early.

Form time was usually the worst bit of the day because Anna didn't have anyone to sit next to. But today she was so excited about going home and seeing Alfie that she didn't even mind about the empty seat beside her. But when Miss Phelps started talking, Anna's heart sank.

"Good news, everyone," she declared.
"We're going to have a special morning
assembly next week to celebrate the
Harvest Festival – and this year we're ALL
going to be involved!"

Anna hid behind her hair as Miss
Phelps walked round the room, putting a
flyer on everyone's desk. "There's a note
there for you to take home,
and your lines for
you to learn,"
she said. "All
the parents
are invited,
and every
single one
of you is
going to
have a part
to play.

We're going to have to practise speaking LOUDLY and CLEARLY so everyone can hear." Anna looked at the words her teacher wanted her to say in front of everyone and felt a bit sick. If she couldn't even talk to one nice person, like Jeff at Battersea, how was she going to speak in front of a whole room full of people?

Miss Phelps clapped her hands. "Let's run through it now, shall we? We'll take it in turns and go round the class. Bella, you start."

Anna's heart was beating so loudly she could barely hear everyone else as they read out their lines. When the girl closest to her, Mary, stood up and said hers, Anna started feeling panicky. She wished Sophie was sitting next to her. She'd make a joke or something so Anna wouldn't feel so bad.

"Very good!" Miss Phelps said as Mary finished. "Anna, you're next. Nice and loud now." Anna's legs felt wobbly as she walked to the front of the class.

Everyone was looking at her. Anna
ducked her head and stared at the card,
but the letters suddenly didn't make any
sense. She wiped her glasses and blinked
at it again, reading the words through in
her head.

At Harvest time there is lots of food. There are crops in the fields and fruit on the trees. Harvest is a time to be thankful for what we have.

Anna's face felt hot as everyone waited for her to say something. Miss Phelps nodded encouragingly.

"At Harvest . . ." Anna started, but her voice sounded like a strangled croak. "At Harvest-time-there-is-lots-of-food . . ." she mumbled without pausing between the words. " . . . to-be-thankful-for-what-we-have," she finished in a rush.

"Well done, Anna," Miss Phelps smiled, "but a little bit too fast. Maybe you could work on it at home? We need everyone to say their lines clearly – there will be lots of people watching."

Anna sat quietly as the rest of the class said their lines. None of them went bright red and stumbled over their words. When the bell rang,

everyone was talking excitedly about the
Harvest Festival as they left the
classroom. But Anna hung her head and
rushed outside as fast as she could. Mum
and Alfie were waiting in the playground.

"What's up?" Mum asked when she
saw Anna's face. Anna shook her head
and bent down to hug Alfie. *I can't
talk in front of everyone*, she
thought, *I just can't!*
Alfie snuggled
into her arms
and licked
her face.

They walked home in silence. Alfie
seemed to know that Anna was upset,
and he stuck close to her side. When they
got in, Mum made Anna sit on the sofa
and tell her what was wrong. Anna
explained about the Harvest Festival.

"I can't do it!" Anna cried. "Sophie
would have loved it. She should do it and
I'll go to France instead."

"It'll be OK," Mum promised. "We'll practise lots. You can read it to me and Alfie – we'll be your audience. And then when it comes to doing it in front of everyone all you need to do is look at us and say it as if we're at home. Either that or imagine everyone in their pants."

"In their *pants*?" Anna laughed.

"Yes," Mum said, trying to keep a straight face. "When you're worried about talking to people, you're supposed to imagine them in their pants. Then they don't seem so scary."

"I can't do that either!" Anna smiled.

"Better go and learn your lines then," Mum told her. "Take Alfie up to your room and practise saying the words to him."

Anna ran upstairs with Alfie trotting at her heels.

She sat opposite Alfie on her bed and
read her words out loud. When she
finished she looked down at her puppy.
He was panting and wagging his tail. He
scrambled down the
bed and landed
in her lap.

"Oh Alfie!" Anna cried, hugging the little dog tight. "It's OK saying my words to you, but it's different talking in front of lots of people." Alfie snuggled closer into her and she stroked his ears. "Nobody minds that you don't speak," she whispered into his fur. "Why can't it be the same for me?"

The Harvest Festival

Anna sat at the bottom of the stairs, tying her shoelaces. Her tummy was tied in knots too, because it was the day of the Harvest Festival assembly and she was petrified! *What if I get my lines wrong?* she thought. *What if I open my mouth and nothing comes out?*

"Are you ready, Anna?" Mum called.

Anna gave her a wobbly smile.

"You can do it."
Mum sat down on
the stairs next to
her and gave
her a hug.
"Just go up
there and do
your best."

Anna stared at
her feet. Alfie sat
looking up at them and wagging his tail.
Anna picked up his
squeaky bone and
threw it for
him. Alfie
dashed after
it, then
trotted back
and dropped it
in front of her.

Anna picked it up
again, and
suddenly Alfie
made a small
grumbly
sound. Anna
and Mum
looked at each
other in amazement.

"Was that Alfie – or was it your
tummy again?" Mum joked.

"It was Alfie!" Anna said in surprise.

She picked him up
and put him on
her lap. He
stared at her
with his
shining black
eyes. "*Rrrruf!*"
he said again.

"Alfie!" Anna hugged him. "You *can* bark, after all!"

"It looks like he's found his voice – even though it *is* a very small one!" Mum laughed.

Anna hugged Alfie's warm body closer to hers. "If you can talk, Alfie, maybe I can too," she said bravely. Alfie licked her under her chin.

"Ready?" Mum asked kindly. Anna gave a small nod.

They walked to school, and Anna said her lines out loud as she went. Alfie ran along next to her, practising his new yappy growl.

When they got into the playground
Mum gave Anna one last hug and went
to join all the other parents, who were
making their way into the hall. Alfie
yapped goodbye as Anna went in. When
she reached the corridor that led to the
hall, everyone else in her class was
already there, talking excitedly. They had
to walk to the front of the hall one by
one until they were standing in a long
row. Then they'd say their lines one after
the other. It would be Anna's turn
after Daniel, and she was just
before Tamsin, who was
standing next to her
looking nervous
too.

They all waited
in silence while
the reception
class, who were
dressed as
vegetables, sang
a song about
farmers. As they

finished their song and everyone clapped,
Anna's stomach lurched. It was her turn.
She looked out on the sea of faces. There
were so many people she couldn't even
see Mum and Alfie.

She scanned the faces desperately, as the
girl on the end, Victoria, said her words.
The words rippled closer and closer to her
as each person in her class said their
part. Soon Daniel was speaking. Anna's
heart was beating really hard, and her
tummy was fluttering.

Suddenly Daniel finished. It was
Anna's turn! The hall was silent as

everyone in it waited for her to speak.
Anna froze. She couldn't remember her
lines. She couldn't think of anything
when there were so many people looking
at her. Someone in the audience coughed.
Anna felt like she was going to cry.

"Anna!" Tamsin whispered. But there
was nothing Anna could do. She opened
her mouth, but no words came out.

Suddenly there was a noise from the audience – a little growly yap. It was Alfie! *"Rruf!"* he barked, over and over again. Anna looked for him and saw him right at the front, jumping up and down on Mum's lap. The old lady next to Mum was tutting crossly, but Mum was ignoring her and smiling at Anna encouragingly. She had her fingers tightly crossed.

"*Rruf! Rruf!*" Alfie barked as if he was saying "*You can do it, Anna!*" Mum gave a nod. "At harvest time," she mouthed to Anna.

Anna gave a watery smile. She looked at Alfie and Mum and pretended that she was saying the words just to them. She said them as loudly and clearly as she could, just as she had in her bedroom. "At Harvest time there is lots of food," she announced. "There are crops in the fields, and fruit on the trees. Harvest is a time to be thankful for what we have." *And I know what I'm thankful for*, Anna thought to herself. *Mum and Alfie!*

Anna could see Mum giving her a thumbs-up and a huge smile. Anna grinned back. She'd done it! The rest of the assembly passed by in a rush. As soon as it was over, Anna rushed out into the playground to see Mum and Alfie. Alfie jumped up at her legs and barked happily. Now the little puppy had found his voice he didn't seem to want to stop!

Anna bent down and picked him up. Mum hugged them both. "I am so proud of you!" she told Anna as she showered kisses down on her head.

"Alfie helped me!" Anna smiled.

"And I've got a surprise for you." Mum grinned even more. "Sophie's mum says that Sophie's been missing you so much she's going to come and stay with us for a week in the October half term. Then she can meet Alfie too!"

"REALLY?" Anna cried.

"Yep!" Mum nodded. "It's all arranged."

"Did you hear that, Alfie? You're going to meet Sophie!" Anna said, stroking his furry head.

"*Rrruf!*" Alfie barked excitedly.

"Oh! Is that Alfie?" came a voice from across the playground. Anna turned to see Tamsin rushing towards her.

"Yes," Anna said shyly. Tamsin came over and looked at the pup in Anna's arms. "Can I stroke him?" she asked excitedly.

"Yes. He likes being tickled just here,"
Anna showed Tamsin the place
behind Alfie's velvety
ears. Alfie wriggled
happily and
turned to lick
Tamsin's
fingers.
Tamsin
squealed in
excitement.

Anna suddenly
had an idea. She still felt shy, but if she'd
just spoken to a whole room full of
people, she could talk to Tamsin! "Would
. . ." she asked. "Would you like to come
round to my house and play with him
one day?"

"Oh, yes please!" Tamsin replied.
"That would be brilliant!"

Mum smiled. "I'll talk to your mum, Tamsin, and we'll sort something out," she promised. "Now, you two had better go in for lunch."

"Do you want to sit with me?" Tamsin asked Anna.

Anna was so pleased that all she could do was nod. Lots of nice things were happening, and it was all because of Alfie. Getting a puppy was the best thing that had ever happened to her!

"Thanks, Alfie!" Anna whispered into Alfie's fur, as she handed him over to Mum.

"*Rruf!*" Alfie replied.

Read on for lots more . . .

🐾 🐾 🐾 🐾

Battersea Dogs & Cats Home

Battersea Dogs & Cats Home is a charity that aims never to turn away a dog or cat in need of our help. We reunite lost dogs and cats with their owners; when we can't do this, we care for them until new homes can be found for them; and we educate the public about responsible pet ownership. Every year the Home takes in around 10,500 dogs and cats. In addition to the site in southwest London, the Home also has two other centres based at Old Windsor, Berkshire, and Brands Hatch, Kent.

The original site in Holloway

History

The Temporary Home for Lost and Starving Dogs was originally opened in a stable yard in Holloway in 1860 by Mary Tealby after she found a starving puppy in the street. There was no one to look after him, so she took him home and nursed him back to health. She was so worried about the other dogs wandering the streets that she opened the Temporary Home for Lost and Starving Dogs. The Home was established to help to look after them all and find them new owners.

Sadly Mary Tealby died in 1865, aged sixty-four, and little more is known about her, but her good work was continued. In 1871 the Home moved to its present site in Battersea, and was renamed the Dogs' Home Battersea.

Some important dates for the Home:

1883 – Battersea start taking in cats.

1914 – 100 sledge dogs are housed at the Hackbridge site, in preparation for Ernest Shackleton's second Antarctic expedition.

1956 – Queen Elizabeth II becomes patron of the Home.

2004 – Red the Lurcher's night-time antics become world famous when he is caught on camera regularly escaping from his kennel and liberating his canine chums for midnight feasts.

2007 – The BBC broadcast *Animal Rescue Live* from the Home for three weeks from mid-July to early August.

Amy Watson

Amy Watson has been working at
Battersea Dogs & Cats Home for six years
and has been the Home's Education
Officer for two and a half years. Amy's
role means that she organizes all the
school visits to the Home for children
aged sixteen and under, and regularly
visits schools around Battersea's three

sites to teach children how to behave and stay safe around dogs and cats, and all about responsible dog and cat ownership. She also regularly features on the Battersea website – www.battersea.org.uk – giving tips and advice on how to train your dog or cat under the "Fun and Learning" section.

On most school visits Amy can take a dog with her, so she is normally accompanied by her beautiful ex-Battersea dog, Hattie. Hattie has been living with Amy for just over a year and really enjoys meeting new children and helping Amy with her work.

The process for re-homing a dog or a cat

When a lost dog or cat arrives, Battersea's Lost Dogs & Cats Line works hard to try to find the animal's owners. If, after seven days, they have not been able to reunite them, the search for a new home can begin.

The Home works hard to find caring, permanent new homes for all the lost and unwanted dogs and cats.

Dogs and cats have their own characters and so staff at the Home will spend time getting to know every dog and cat. This helps decide the type of home the dog or cat needs.

There are three stages of the re-homing process at Battersea Dogs & Cats Home. Battersea's re-homing team wants to find you the perfect pet: sometimes this can take a while, so please be patient while we search for your new friend!

1 Register details

2 Match

3 Leaving with your new pet

Have a look at our website: **http://www.battersea.org.uk/dogs/ rehoming/index.html** for more details!

"Did you know?" questions about dogs and cats

- Puppies do not open their eyes until they are about two weeks old.

- According to *Guinness World Records*, the smallest living dog is a long-haired Chihuahua called Danka Kordak from Slovakia, who is 13.8cm tall and 18.8cm long.

- Dalmatians, with all those cute black spots, are actually born white.

- The greyhound is the fastest dog on earth. It can reach speeds of up to 45 miles per hour.

- The first living creature sent into space was a female dog named Laika.

- Cats spend 15% of their day grooming themselves and a massive 70% of their day sleeping.

- Cats see six times better in the dark than we do.

- A cat's tail helps it to balance when it is on the move – especially when it is jumping.

- The cat, giraffe and camel are the only animals that walk by moving both their left feet, then both their right feet, when walking.

Dos and Don'ts of looking after dogs and cats

Dogs dos and don'ts

DO

- Be gentle and quiet around dogs at all times – treat them how you would like to be treated.
- Have respect for dogs.

DON'T

- Sneak up on a dog – you could scare them.
- Tease a dog – it's not fair.
- Stare at a dog – dogs can find this scary.
- Disturb a dog who is sleeping or eating.

- Assume a dog wants to play with you. Just like you, sometimes they may want to be left alone.
- Approach a dog who is without an owner as you won't know if the dog is friendly or not.

Cats dos and don'ts

DO
- Be gentle and quiet around cats at all times.
- Have respect for cats.
- Let a cat approach you in their own time.

DON'T
- Never stare at a cat as they can find this intimidating.

- Tease a cat – it's not fair.
- Disturb a sleeping or eating cat – they may not want attention or to play.
- Assume a cat will always want to play. Like you, sometimes they want to be left alone.

Some fun pet-themed puzzles!

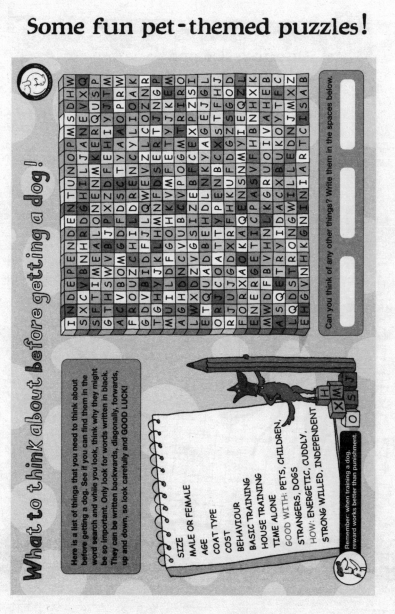

What to think about before getting a dog!

Here is a list of things that you need to think about before getting a dog. See if you can find them in the word search and while you look, think why they might be so important. Only look for words written in black. They can be written backwards, diagonally, forwards, up and down, so look carefully and GOOD LUCK!

SIZE
MALE OR FEMALE
AGE
COAT TYPE
COST
BEHAVIOUR
BASIC TRAINING
HOUSE TRAINING
TIME ALONE
GOOD WITH: PETS, CHILDREN, STRANGERS, DOGS
HOW: ENERGETIC, CUDDLY, STRONG WILLED, INDEPENDENT

Remember: when training a dog, reward works better than punishment.

Can you think of any other things? Write them in the spaces below.

Tangled Leads and Crazy Maze

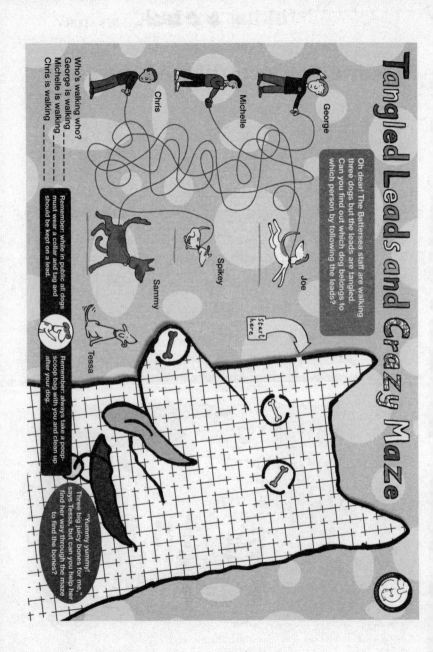

Oh dear! The Battersea staff are walking three dogs but the leads are tangled. Can you find out which dog belongs to which person by following the leads?

George

Michelle

Chris

Joe

Spikey

Sammy

Tessa

start here

Who's walking who?

George is walking ----
Michelle is walking ----
Chris is walking ----

Remember: while in public all dogs must wear a collar and tag and should be kept on a lead.

Remember: always take a poop-scoop bag with you and clean up after your dog.

"Yummy yummy! Three big juicy bones for me." says Tessa, but can you help her find her way through the maze to find the bones?

Making a Mask

Copy these faces onto a piece of paper and
ask an adult to help you cut them out.

Here is a delicious recipe for you to follow.

Remember to ask an adult to help you.

Cheddar Cheese Dog Cookies

You will need:

227g grated Cheddar cheese
(use at room temperature)

114g margarine

1 egg

1 clove of garlic (crushed)

172g wholewheat flour

30g wheatgerm

1 teaspoon salt

30ml milk

Preheat the oven to 375°F/190°C/gas mark 5.

Cream the cheese and margarine together.

When smooth, add the egg and garlic and mix well. Add the flour, wheatgerm and salt. Mix well until a dough forms. Add the milk and mix again.

Chill the mixture in the fridge for one hour.

Roll the dough onto a floured surface until it is about 4cm thick. Use cookie cutters to cut out shapes.

Bake on an ungreased baking tray for 15–18 minutes.

Cool to room temperature and store in an airtight container in the fridge.

There are lots of fun things on the
website, including an online quiz, e-cards,
colouring sheets and recipes for making
dog and cat treats.

www.battersea.org.uk